D0769714

Wiley and the Hairy Man

ADAPTED FROM AN AMERICAN FOLK TALE

by Molly Garrett Bang

Ready-to-Read
Aladdin Paperbacks

Acknowledgments:
Thanks to *Swallow* and the Trailside Museum

This folktale is based on "Wiley and the Hairy Man," as recorded
by Donnell Van de Voort in "Manuscripts of the Federal Writers'
Project of the Works Progress Administration for the state of
Alabama" and published in *A Treasury of American Folklore*,
edited by B. A. Botkin.

First Aladdin Paperbacks Edition, 1987
Copyright ©1976 by Molly Bang

Aladdin Paperbacks
An imprint of Simon & Schuster Children's Publishing Division
1230 Avenue of the Americas
New York, NY 10020

All rights reserved including the right of reproduction in whole or
in part in any form.

READY-TO-READ is a registered trademark of Simon & Schuster, Inc.

Also available in a Simon & Schuster Books for Young Readers Edition.

Printed and bound in the United States of America

10 9 8 7 6 5 4 3 2 1

The Library of Congress has cataloged the hardcover edition as follows:

Bang, Molly.
Wiley and the Hairy Man.
(Ready-to-read)
Summary: With his mother's help, Wiley outwits the hairy creature that
dominates the swamp near his home by the Tombigbee River.
[1. Folklore—United States] I. Title. II. Series
[PZ8.1.B228Wi 1987] 398.2'1'0973 [E] 87-2540

ISBN: 1-4169-9843-8 ISBN-13: 978-1-4169-9843-3

FOR MY PARENTS

It was a long time ago.

Wiley and his mother

lived near a swamp.

The swamp was near

the Tombigbee River.

One day Wiley wanted

to cut some bamboo.

He needed poles for the hen roost.

He got his ax to go down to the swamp.

Wiley's mother said,
"Wiley, be careful
when you go to the swamp.
Take your hound dogs with you.
The Hairy Man will get you
if you don't watch out."

Wiley's mother knew
the Hairy Man hated hound dogs.
She knew because she knew all
about the ways of the swamp.
She had grown up on
the Tombigbee River.

Wiley said,

"I'll watch out.

I'll take my hound dogs with me

everywhere I go."

But when he got to the swamp,

his dogs saw a wild pig.

They ran after it.

They ran so far away Wiley

couldn't even hear them yelp.

"Well," thought Wiley,

"I hope the Hairy Man

isn't anywhere around here."

He took his ax

and began cutting poles.

When Wiley looked up,
there was the Hairy Man.
He was coming through the
trees. He sure was ugly.
He was hairy all over.
His eyes burned like coals.
His teeth were big
and sharp and white.
He was swinging a sack.

Wiley was scared.
Quick as he could,
he climbed up a
big bay tree.
Wiley had seen that
the Hairy Man had
feet like a cow.
And Wiley knew
a cow could not
climb a tree.

The Hairy Man stood
at the foot of the tree.
He called,
"Wiley, what are you
doing up there?"
Wiley said,
"My mother told me
to stay away from you."

Then Wiley asked,
"What's in your
big old sack?"
"Nothing yet,"
the Hairy Man said.
He picked up Wiley's ax
and began to chop down
the tree.

Wiley held tight to the tree.

He rubbed his belly against it.

Then he hollered,

"Fly, chips, fly!

Fly back to your same old place!"

The chips flew back.

The Hairy Man chopped faster.

Wiley hollered as fast as he could.

But the Hairy Man was faster.

The chips flew and flew.

The Hairy Man was winning.

Then from 'way far off,

Wiley heard his hound dogs yelping.

"H-E-R-E, dogs!" he hollered.

The dogs came running.

As soon as the Hairy Man saw them,

he fled away into the swamp.

When Wiley got home,
he told his mother
what had happened.
"Did the Hairy Man have his sack
with him?" she asked.
"Yes, ma'am, he did," said Wiley.

"Well," his mother said,
"the next time the Hairy Man
    comes after you, don't climb a tree.
    Just stay on the ground and say,
    'Hello, Hairy Man.'
    The Hairy Man will say,
    'Hello, Wiley.'

"Then you say,
'I hear you're the best
conjure man around here.'"
"What's 'conjure'?"
Wiley asked his mother.
She answered,
"It's magic."

She went on,
"You tell him he is the best
conjure man, and he'll say,
'I reckon I am.'
Then you say,
'I bet you can't
change yourself
into a giraffe.'
And he will
change himself
into a giraffe.

"Then you say,
'I bet you can't change yourself
into an alligator.'
And he will change himself
into an alligator.
You keep telling him
what he can't do.
He'll keep doing it
just to show you.

"Then you say,
'Everybody can change
into something BIG.
I bet you can't change yourself
into a little possum.'
He will change into
a little possum.
You grab him right away
and throw him into his sack.
Then you take the sack
and throw it into the river."

Wiley was scared to do
what his mother said.
But the next time he had
to go to the swamp,
he tied up his hound dogs.

As soon as he got to the swamp,

Wiley saw the Hairy Man.

He was coming at him through the trees.

He was swinging his sack.

He was grinning because he knew

Wiley had left his hound dogs behind.

Wiley wanted to run away,

but he stayed there.

He said, "Hello, Hairy Man."

And the Hairy Man said, "Hello, Wiley."

"Hairy Man," said Wiley,

"I hear you're the best

conjure man around here."

"I reckon I am," said the Hairy Man.

"I bet you can't change yourself
  into a giraffe," said Wiley.
"Sure I can," the Hairy Man said.
"That's no trouble at all."
The Hairy Man twisted around,
  and he changed himself into a giraffe.

Then Wiley said,
"I bet you can't change yourself
into an alligator."
The giraffe twisted around
and changed itself
into an alligator.

So Wiley said,
"Everybody can change
into something BIG.
I bet you can't change yourself
into a little possum."
The alligator twisted around
and changed itself
into a little possum.
Wiley grabbed the possum
and threw it into the
Hairy Man's sack.

He tied the sack as tight as he could.
Then he threw the sack into
the Tombigbee River.
Wiley started back home
through the swamp.
He felt happy.

But he hadn't gone far, when

there was the Hairy Man again.

He was coming at Wiley.

Wiley climbed right up the nearest tree.

"How did you get out?"

he called down to the Hairy Man.

"I changed myself into the wind,"

said the Hairy Man,

"and I blew my way out.

Now I'm going to wait right down here.

You'll get hungry,

and you'll come down

out of that tree."

Wiley thought and thought.
He thought about the
Hairy Man waiting below.
He thought about his
hound dogs tied up at home.
After a while Wiley said,
"Hairy Man, you did some
pretty good tricks.
But I bet you can't
make things disappear."
The Hairy Man said,
"Ha! That's what I'm best at.
See the bird's nest on that branch?"
Wiley looked. It was there.
Then it was gone.

But Wiley said,

"I never saw it in the first place.

I bet you can't make something

I know is there disappear."

"Look at your shirt, Wiley,"

the Hairy Man said.

Wiley looked down.

His shirt was gone!

"Oh, that was just a plain old shirt,"

he said. "But this rope

around my pants is magic.

My mother conjured it.

I bet you can't make

this rope disappear."

The Hairy Man said, "I can make all
the rope in this county disappear."
"I bet you can't," said Wiley.
The Hairy Man threw out his chest.
He opened his mouth wide
and he hollered loud,
"All the rope in this county,
DISAPPEAR!"

The rope around Wiley's pants was gone.

He held his pants up with one hand.

He held on to the tree with the other,

and he hollered loud,

"H-E-R-E, dogs!"

The dogs came running,

and the Hairy Man fled away.

When Wiley got home, he told
his mother what had happened.
"Well," she said,
"you fooled the Hairy Man twice.
If we can fool him one more time,
he'll never come back
to bother us again.
But he'll be mighty hard to fool
the third time."

Wiley's mother sat down
in her rocking chair
and she thought.

Wiley couldn't sit still.

He went outside

and tied up one dog

at the front door.

He tied up the other dog

at the back door.

Then he came inside.

He crossed a broom and an ax

over the window.

He built a fire in the fireplace.

Then he sat down

and helped his mother think.

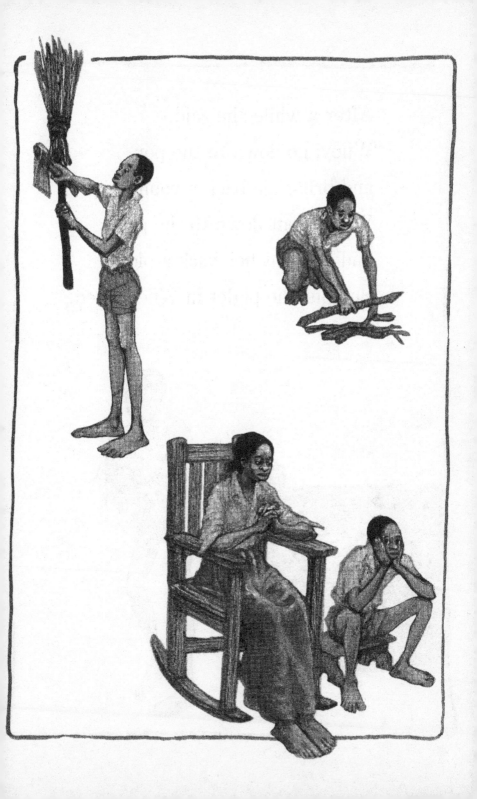

After a while she said,
"Wiley, go down to the pen
and bring me back a young pig."
Wiley went down to the pen
and brought her back a piglet.
She put the piglet in Wiley's bed.

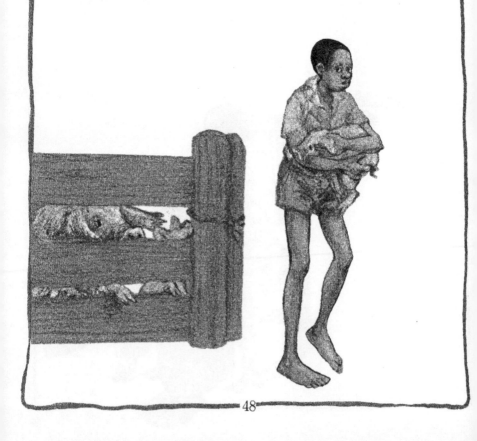

His mother said,
"Wiley, you go up
to the loft and hide."
Wiley climbed up
to the loft.

He looked out front
through a knothole in a plank.
He saw a great big animal
run out of the swamp toward the house.
The dog out front broke loose.
It chased the animal
back into the swamp.

Wiley looked out back through
a crack between the planks.
He saw another animal run out of
the swamp toward the house.
The other dog broke loose.
It chased the animal
back into the swamp.

The wind howled and the house shook.
Wiley heard footsteps on the roof
over his head. It was the Hairy Man.
He was trying to come down
the chimney. When the Hairy Man
touched the chimney and found
it was hot, he cursed and swore.
Then he jumped down from the roof,
and he walked right up to the front door.
He banged on it and yelled out,
"Momma, I've come for your young'un!"
But Wiley's mother called back,
"You can't have him, Hairy Man!"

The Hairy Man said,

"I'll set your house on fire with lightning.

I'll burn it down

if you don't give him to me!"

But Wiley's mother called back,
"I have plenty of
sweet milk, Hairy Man.
The milk will
put out your fire."

Then the Hairy Man said,

"I'll dry up your cow.

I'll dry up your spring.

I'll send a million boll weevils

out of the ground

to eat up your cotton

if you don't give me your young'un."

"Hairy Man," said Wiley's mother,

"you wouldn't do all that.

That's mighty mean."

"I'm a mighty mean man,"

said the Hairy Man.

So Wiley's mother said,
"If I do give you the young'un,
will you go away
and never come back?"
"I swear I will," said
the Hairy Man.

Wiley's mother opened the door.

"He's over in that bed," she said.

The Hairy Man grinned and grinned.

He walked over to the bed.

He snatched the covers back.

"Hey!" he yelled.

"There's nothing in this bed
  but a young pig!"

"I never said which young'un
  I'd give you,"
  Wiley's mother answered.

The Hairy Man stomped his feet.

He gnashed his teeth.

He raged and yelled.

Then he grabbed the piglet
and fled away with it into the swamp.

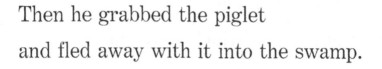

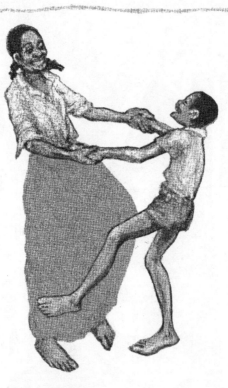

Wiley came down from the loft.

"Is the Hairy Man gone for good?"

"He sure is," said Wiley's mother.

"He can't ever get you now."

Wiley and his mother had fooled
the Hairy Man three times,
and they never saw him again.